KamA
THE FACELESS BEAST

THE DARKEST HOUR

KamA
THE FACELESS
BEAST

With special thanks to Allan Frewin Jones

www.beastquest.co.uk

ORCHARD BOOKS
338 Euston Road, London NW1 3BH
Orchard Books Australia
Level 17/207 Kent St, Sydney, NSW 2000

A Paperback Original
First published in Great Britain in 2013

A CIP catalogue record for this book is available from
the British Library.

ISBN 978 1 40832 401 1

1 3 5 7 9 10 8 6 4 2

Printed and bound by CPI Group (UK) Ltd, Croydon, CR0 4YY

The paper and board used in this paperback are natural recyclable
products made from wood grown in sustainable forests. The
manufacturing processes conform to the environmental regulations of
the country of origin.

Orchard Books is a division of Hachette Children's Books,
an Hachette UK company

www.hachette.co.uk

THE ICY DESERT

KAYONIAN MARSHLANDS

MEATON

THE CITY

ERRINEL

Dear Reader,

My hand shakes as I write. You find us in our hour of greatest peril.

My master Aduro has been snatched away. The kingdom is on its knees. Not one, but two enemies circle our shores – Kensa, the banished witch, has returned from Henkrall. With her stalks Sanpao, the Pirate King. Strange magic is afoot, stirring not just in Avantia but all the kingdoms, and I sense new Beasts lurking.

Only Tom and Elenna stand in the way of certain destruction. Can they withstand the awful test that will surely come? This time, courage alone may have to be enough.

Yours, in direst straits,

Daltec the apprentice

PROLOGUE

"There it goes again," muttered Tess, peering up into the blue sky. Her eyes squinted against the searing forks of lightning. She looked fearfully at her friend Maria. "I tell you, it's not natural to have lightning on a cloudless day."

Maria stared up at the crackling sky. "It's strange," she said, "but it's doing us no harm."

Tess shook her head. "Unnatural, I call it," she insisted. "Sinister."

Maria gave a brief laugh. "You let your imagination run away with you, Tess," she said. If bad magic were working in the realm, Maria felt sure her nephew Tom would know how to deal with it. At least, she hoped he would. "Come along," she said. "Let's pick up the grain we need and get back home before the rain starts."

The grain store was in a large network of caves on the outskirts of the village. The caves kept the grain cool and dry, and they weren't far away, but today Maria felt every step dragging. Where was her beloved nephew? He had spent many long months fighting the evil magic and the monstrous Beasts that it spawned.

Is he even in Avantia? she wondered fretfully. *Or is he battling Beasts in some distant realm?*

A wicker screen covered the entrance to the grain cave, put there to keep scavengers out. They took away the stones that held it in place and slid it aside.

The cave mouth was low and narrow. Lanterns stood just inside. Maria worked tinder and flint to create a flame, and lit two of the lanterns.

She handed one lantern to Tess, and raised the other in front of her. The light revealed a short curved tunnel. Beyond it, the cave opened out into a honeycomb of chambers, filled with wooden grain barrels.

"Pooh!" said Tess, wrinkling her nose. "That's a bad smell, and no mistake!"

Maria moved along the short tunnel. She could smell it too – a sharp, bitter odour that tickled in her nose and made her want to cough.

"It smells like meat that's fallen into the fire," Tess said uneasily.

Yes, that's it, thought Maria. *The reek of burned flesh.*

But there was no meat kept here, and even if there were, this was no place to cook it.

Suspicious and with her nerves tingling, Maria led her friend to the end of the tunnel. They turned the corner.

"What is this?" gasped Maria in alarm as the light shone on a silky blanket of dense spider's webs, stretching from roof to floor along both sides of the cave. The webs were so thick that she could barely see the grain barrels hidden beneath.

"By King Hugo's crown!" cried

Tess. "It must have taken a thousand spiders months on end to weave such webs!"

"That's impossible," said Maria, shuddering. "Our people come here almost every day. Someone would have spoken of an infestation of spiders."

No, horrifying as it might seem, these webs must have been spun overnight, Maria realised.

And that meant only one thing. The web-weaver was not a normal spider.

"Let's go," she said, struggling to keep her voice calm and level, anxious to get her friend to safety.

But she was too late. Before either of them could move, a large, sinister shape scuttled forwards out of the darkness.

Tess let out a scream that echoed

through the caves. Maria stared at the approaching Beast, the lantern shaking in her hand, her blood running cold.

Its lower half was in deep shadow, but from the waist up it had the form of a muscular man. Thick veins ran under his dark skin. Long, oily black hair hung over its wide shoulders and veiled its face so that only one terrible eye was visible.

Maria saw that the powerful chest and arms were covered in hideous burns, open and raw. Now she knew the source of the sickening smell! There was a long, diagonal scar down its chest, as though a sword had cut deep into its flesh.

Maria fought against a dreadful dizziness as the Beast moved towards her and the full horror of

its appearance was revealed. Its
lower body was that of a huge, hairy
spider. Its bloated belly hung down
between eight spindly, crooked legs
as it scuttled forwards on knife-sharp
points.

The Beast lifted its right arm and

Maria saw that a length of thick, twined web hung like a whip from its raised fist.

Maria turned and pushed at Tess. "Run!"

Wailing with terror, Tess darted for the cave entrance. Maria was close behind, but as she stumbled along, she felt something sticky wrap around her ankle. She toppled forwards, grazing her hands on the rough ground.

Gasping from the fall, she saw Tess run around the corner and out of sight. Maria's lantern lay on the ground, but its flame still flickered, and by the feeble light she saw that the Beast's whip had coiled around her ankle.

Maria screamed as she was dragged

backwards, away from the light and into the black depths of the caves.

Tom, Tom, where are you?

CHAPTER ONE

FLIGHT INTO DOOM

"Dok?" Tom did his best to keep the frustration out of his voice. "How much longer is this going to take?"

The Kayonian scientist popped his head up over the rim of his strange flying machine, his wild hair framing his face. "It's almost ready," he said, jumping out and pulling a length of rope towards a large wooden cart.

"If we're to take your horse with us to Avantia, we must have a suitable carrier for him, mustn't we?"

"Of course," Tom agreed. "I won't go back to my homeland without Storm. But Kensa and Sanpao are on their way to attack Avantia. We have to get going."

They had only just returned to the city of Meaton after a hard-won victory over Mirka the Ice-Horse.

"Is there anything we can do to help speed things up?" asked Elenna.

"It'll be ready soon," muttered Dok. He attached the rope to the cart then jumped back into the flying machine. "I just have to make sure the burners are fully functional."

A low rumbling noise echoed through the city and the ground trembled under Tom's feet. *Another earthquake!*

"Now that five of the six Evil Beasts are gone, the kingdoms are returning to their proper places," he said. "Which means Avantia is moving further away all the time."

The terrible power of the Lightning Beasts let loose by Kensa's sorceries had warped the various realms, crushing them together and creating terror and mayhem.

But that was not Tom's only concern: the Circle of Wizards had charged him with a mission to track down and capture Kensa and Sanpao. Although Tom had defeated the Beasts so far, the evil duo was still at large. If he failed in his mission, the Good Wizard Aduro would never be released from imprisonment.

Would Dok's machine ever be ready?

"Almost done," Dok said. "I just have to get one last thing." He scuttled off and disappeared into Queen Romaine's castle.

"Now what?" groaned Elenna.

Tom was about to chase after the scientist when Dok reappeared with two of Queen Romaine's soldiers.

They were carrying what looked like a pair of wide metal wings.

"For added speed," Dok explained. "You'll thank me for it later!" He instructed the soldiers on how to fix the wings onto the sides of the basket, and then attached metal cables from them to the burners.

"All done," Dok said. "Everyone aboard." He turned valves at the bottom of the burners and two gusts of bright red flame shot upwards.

The billowing canopy of rare Kayonian silk began to fill with heated air. With a creaking and straining of wicker and of ropes, the machine shifted on the ground.

Tom guided Storm into the large cart and secured its high sides, while Elenna and Silver the wolf leaped into the basket next to Dok.

"I hope Dok's right about this being safe," Tom muttered as he clambered in with the others. A moment later, the flying machine left the ground and rose rapidly into the sky.

Tom leaned over the side. Storm's cart was swinging a little at the end of its rope, but the brave horse didn't seem to be frightened. "Good boy!" Tom called down. "Everything will be fine."

"So, my friends," said Dok, his eyes shining. "I've never been beyond Kayonia's borders before. Which way to Avantia's capital city?"

"First we should check for Beasts," said Tom, taking the magical parchment map from his tunic and unrolling it. "If the map shows... Oh!"

"What is it?" asked Elenna.

Tom stared at the mystical three-dimensional representation of mountains and forests and plains. A new pathway shone out, leading directly to Tom's home village of Errinel. He looked at Dok. "Set a course south-east," he cried. "My aunt and uncle are in danger!"

He stared at the name inscribed above the village. *Kama*. A cold chill ran down his back. *What was this creature that had descended on his village?*

Dok worked the flying machine's controls and the great metal wings began to beat, sending them scudding through the air at a remarkable speed. Tom watched the city of Meaton shrink and vanish into the distance behind them.

Silver whined a little, crouching down at Elenna's feet.

"He doesn't like heights," she murmured, stroking his head to calm him.

The flying machine burst out

through a canopy of white clouds and they sailed on in bright sunshine. Tom stared down in amazement as the Icy Plains fled away beneath them and they crossed over into the mountainous north of Avantia.

Glancing back, Tom found he could no longer see Kayonia. "The World of Chaos has returned to its proper place," he said. "We only just made the crossing in time."

He stared southwards, aching for the first sight of the village where he had been born. *At this speed, we'll be there in no time!*

But then the flying machine lurched and the burners coughed and gushed thin grey smoke.

"Curses!" cried Dok. "We're running low on fuel – once my supply of firedrake's blood is gone, we will fall from the sky!"

The machine shuddered again and dropped with a sickening lurch.

"Isn't there anything we can do?" shouted Tom.

"Not unless we find another fuel source," called Dok, wrestling with the controls. "A bolt or two of lightning might add enough power, but where are we to find lightning in a clear blue sky?"

Tom stared at Elenna, and saw that she was looking at the pouch at his waist that contained the last Lightning Token.

"Could we use this?" asked Tom, taking out the orb marked with a lightning fork.

"But don't we need it to battle the final Beast?" asked Elenna.

"There won't be a battle if we

crash," said Tom.

Already Storm's cart was skimming the higher peaks. At any moment the flying machine could smash into a mountainside and they would all tumble to their deaths.

"We don't have a choice!" Tom shouted above the howl of the wind. *This has to work*, he thought. *Otherwise I've sacrificed the token for nothing.*

He flung the last Lightning Token into the iron grille at the base of the burners.

CHAPTER TWO

DREADFUL TIDINGS

The Lightning Token exploded,
spraying out a shower of red sparks.
Fierce red fire erupted in the base of
the burners and Dok's flying machine
began to rise jerkily into the sky, the
wings flapping strongly as it soared
up over the peaks.

Wind whipped in Tom's hair as the
machine sped along, faster than ever.

He leaned over the side and peered
down. *Yes!* Storm was still safe, braced
against the back of the cart as the
rushing air made his mane and tail
fly.

Tom stared down, past the orchards
and fields, to the familiar cluster of
houses and barns that he had known

all his life. "See the house with the slate roof?" he exclaimed. "That's my Uncle's forge. Land there."

Dok pulled levers and twisted wheels and the flying machine began to descend.

As Storm's cart bumped gently to earth, Tom climbed over the rail and slid down the rope. He led his horse away as the flying machine settled on the ground. Silver leaped out, running in a tight circle, clearly glad to be on firm land again.

"Look after the animals," Tom called to Elenna as he cautiously made his way towards his uncle's workshop. Normally he would have heard the clang and clank of worked iron and the roar of the furnace – but now, the forge was eerily silent.

With his heart beating fast and his

hand on his sword-hilt, Tom peered around the door. His uncle was in there, pacing the floor, his hands wringing his leather apron. Something was wrong.

"What's happened?" Tom asked, running in.

"Tom!" Uncle Henry grasped Tom in his strong arms. "Your aunt is missing," he said. "She went as usual to the grain stores, but she never returned." He shuddered. "Something has taken her and I don't know where to look. There's been lightning in the sky most days," he said. "Evil magic is upon us. It has taken my Maria and I fear that worse is to come."

Tom gazed into his uncle's worried eyes. *It's my fault that this horror has fallen on Avantia. If I hadn't travelled the Lightning Path the Beasts wouldn't have*

*been released and Aunt Maria would
be safe.*

He rested his hand on his uncle's.
"I will find her and bring her back
to you," he promised. "Whatever it
takes."

Tom ran out into the yard at the
back of the forge. "Dok, you need to
leave Avantia as quickly as you can.

There's terrible danger here."

"I have with me the alchemical powders and fluids I need to brew a fresh batch of firedrake's blood," the scientist replied. "It will take a while, but as soon as I've made the mixture, I'll depart."

"Good," said Tom, running to Storm and leaping into the saddle. "Thank you for all of your help. But now, Elenna and I have a Quest to finish!" Storm reared up and whinnied loudly.

Tom helped Elenna up behind him and they set off at a brisk trot with Silver running alongside.

"Did your uncle tell you where the Beast is?" Elenna asked.

"Not exactly," Tom replied. "But my aunt went missing in the grain caves, so we'll head there first."

"You think the Beast has her?" Elenna asked anxiously.

"I do," said Tom.

They rode swiftly out of the village, following a path that led through a dense patch of prickly shrubbery.

Suddenly Silver paused and lifted his head, sniffing the air.

"Maybe he's found Maria's scent," said Elenna.

Tom watched closely as the wolf began to push his way in among the roadside bushes. Dread chilled his heart. Was his aunt lying dead at the side of the road?

"Oh!" cried a shrill voice. "Don't eat me! Mercy!"

Tom sprang down from the saddle, drawing his sword and raking aside a heap of twigs and leafy branches. Lying curled up underneath the

foliage was his aunt's friend, Tess.
She stared in terror into Silver's
yellow eyes.

"Tess, it's me," Tom reassured her,
helping her up. "Silver won't harm
you. Please, I'm looking for my aunt –
do you know what happened to her?"

Tess was shaking with fear. "It was
the thing," she babbled, pointing

towards the caves. "There were webs everywhere… It was huge… Maria told me to run… I thought she was behind me." She put her hands over her face and began to weep. "The horrible spider-thing caught her! I think she's dead!"

CHAPTER THREE

WEBS OF FEAR

Tom stared at Tess in alarm.

She peered at him through her clawed fingers. "It's coming for me, too," she wailed.

"Don't worry," said Elenna. "We won't let anything harm you."

"Go back to Errinel," Tom told the trembling woman. "Silver and Storm will protect you."

Tess reached out a quivering hand

to him. "You were always a good boy, Tom," she said. "But why did you go off gallivanting when your aunt and uncle needed you?"

Tom gave her a helpless look. It would take far too long to explain the importance of his Quests. "I'm back now," he said. "And I don't believe Aunt Maria is dead. Elenna and I are going to rescue her."

He hoped he was right.

Tom and Elenna watched for a few moments as Tess and the two animals made their way back along the narrow path towards Errinel. Then they turned, Tom with his hand on his sword-hilt, Elenna with an arrow ready for her bow, and headed onwards to the caves.

The wicker screen lay beside the cave mouth. Tom assumed that Tess had knocked it over as she'd fled.

"There are lanterns and flints inside," Tom explained to Elenna as she peered nervously into the darkness. *If Kama has hurt Aunt Maria I will never forgive myself.*

They entered and Tom quickly lit a lantern. He gave it to Elenna and drew his sword. He intended to be

ready for whatever was lurking in there.

They were barely six paces along the curved tunnel when a foul stench struck them.

"Yuck!" gasped Elenna, holding her hand to her mouth. "It reminds me of when meat fat gets burned onto the bottom of a cook-pot!"

Tom nodded. "It must be something to do with the Beast," he murmured, trying to breathe as shallowly as possible to keep the vile stink out of his nose.

He drew the ruby of Torgor out of his tunic and focused on it. The red jewel had the power to allow him to communicate with Beasts. An all-too familiar refrain slipped into his mind, darkening his thoughts.

The son of Taladon must die…

Tom winced, taken aback by the spite and venom in the hissing voice. *He shall die at the hands of Kama...*

We'll, see about that, Tom thought, hoping Kama could hear him. *I've been threatened with death many times but I'm still here – unlike the Beasts who threatened me.*

If the Beast was close by, chances were that his Aunt Maria was too. Frightened and helpless. Relying on him to save her. Tom strode on, his shield up, and sword at the ready. "If the Beast has harmed Aunt Maria, it will pay dearly," he said with grim anger.

With Elenna close behind, holding the lantern high, Tom marched between web-shrouded barrels, shuddering a little as he passed under the great hanging curtains of webbing.

As he moved through layer upon layer of sticky grey strands, he felt sure he was walking into a carefully laid snare from which there could be no escape.

He looked back at Elenna. "Try not to touch any of this stuff," he warned her. "You could get caught in it."

He rounded a corner and walked straight into a huge web that had been spun across the tunnel ahead.

"Ugh!" he exclaimed. "I didn't take my own advice."

Elenna ran up behind. "Don't struggle, I'll cut you free," she said. She drew her knife and hacked at the thick webs while he clawed at his face to get the disgusting stuff out of his eyes. The web was tough and springy, but he managed to tear himself clear. As he pulled the last few strands out

of his hair, he was gasping from
the exertion.

More webs confronted them as
they moved along the tunnel, each
one thicker and more treacherous
than the last. But the gauntlets of the
Golden Armour gave Tom the extra
strength he needed to slice through
the webs and open a path for them
to continue.

Hacking through the final layer,
Tom and Elenna found themselves
staring into a vast cavernous space.
It hung with ropes of web and the
air was heavy with the overpowering
stench of burnt flesh.

A hideous cocoon of webbing
leaned against the cavern wall. Tom
gasped as he saw his aunt's ashen face
within.

"She's here!" he cried, leaping

forwards. He bit his lip as he stood
in front of the horrible coffin. *Is she
dead? Have I come too late?*

His aunt's eyes flickered open, and
a faint light of hope ignited in them as
she saw him. Strands of web covered
her mouth, preventing her from
speaking.

How could he cut her free without hurting her?

"Tom!" Elenna's voice was a fearful shriek.

He spun around, his heart hammering as he stared up at the dreadful form that loomed over him.

From the waist down it was a monstrous spider with a bulging, sagging body covered in bristling hair and with spindly, crooked legs that bent high above its head. But its upper parts were formed of the torso, arms and head of a man! A single terrible black eye glared at Tom from behind long lank hair. A muscular arm with horrible burned flesh rose and a long thick whip cracked in the air.

A voice hissed angrily in Tom's head. *The son of Taladon must die!*

CHAPTER FOUR

THE DEADLY CAVERN

Tom ducked as the whip of braided webbing hissed viciously above his head.

Kama let out a high-pitched screech of anger, his two front legs rising to claw the air with razor-sharp barbs.

"Save Aunt Maria!" Tom shouted to Elenna as he sprang aside and raced across the cave to avoid a second lash

of the whip. Kama was very fast as he spun around and scuttled in pursuit.

Kama struck again with the whip and it cracked loudly a fraction above Tom's head as he dived and rolled over the floor. He noticed the black entrance to another tunnel leading from the cavern. Could he lure the

Beast away long enough for Elenna to free his aunt?

He scrambled towards the hole, Kama following on clattering pointed legs.

It's too dark! he thought. In that gloomy tunnel, a darkness-dweller like the Spider Beast would have the advantage. But then Tom thought of the ruby of Torgor. He drew it out again. Sure enough, it gave off a faint red glow.

It will be enough for me to see by, Tom thought as he hurled himself through the entrance. "Hey!" he shouted at the Beast. "Don't dare to follow me, Kama! Your destruction lies in this tunnel!"

With an echoing screech of pure hatred, Kama skittered to the entrance, his eye burning with a loathsome light.

Tom ran as the Beast lunged forwards. But this tunnel was also hung with sticky webs. He thrust and chopped with his sword, pushing onwards. Kama's barbed feet clicked ferociously behind.

Tom risked a glance back and saw the whip was becoming thicker and longer at every lash, as though it were drawing more of the webs into itself.

No more running! Tom said to himself as he turned to face the Beast. The whip sliced through the air, but this time Tom lifted his sword in both hands to try and cut through it.

The whip coiled around the blade, holding it fast.

I hadn't realised it would be so strong! Kama wrenched back on the whip and Tom was dragged almost off his feet. He dug his heels in and pulled back, his teeth gritted, the blood ringing in his ears.

But Kama was powerful. The Beast
gave another tug on the whip and
Tom was thrown forwards onto his
face and his sword almost ripped
from his hands. Tom twisted around,
digging his boots into the side of the
tunnel and tugging with all his might.

It took every ounce of strength left in his arms to tear his blade from the coils of the whip.

"I've cut your aunt loose!" Tom heard Elenna calling. "I'll take her to safety! Then I'll come back to help you!"

"No!" shouted Tom as Kama came hurtling after him. "It's too dangerous! The Beast knows these caves too well!"

That was it! He had been a fool to try and defeat Kama in his own lair. He had to lure the Beast out into the open…

But how?

"Leave me," he heard his aunt's weary voice echoing from the cavern. "Go to Tom's aid! This is the Beast that gave Taladon the hardest battle of his life."

"Get Maria out of here!" Tom yelled. "I know what to do."

Hearing his aunt speak his father's name had given Tom an idea. He closed his fist around the ruby of Torgor, concentrating hard to try and project his voice into the Beast's mind.

"Hear me, Kama!" he said aloud. "I am the son of Taladon, Master of the Beasts! Whatever my father did to you in the past, I vow that I will do a thousand times worse!"

The Beast gave a shivering shriek, his dreadful black eye widening and filling with an evil light of understanding. His whole body shook with rage, his forelegs rising and scratching at the air.

"If you want your revenge," called Tom, "come and do your worst! I do not fear you!"

With an ear-splitting roar of fury, Kama sprang forward to tear Tom to pieces.

CHAPTER FIVE

THE FACELESS BEAST

Tom knew he had to time his next move precisely. As Kama lunged forwards, Tom flung himself under the low belly of the Beast and rolled out behind him.

Not even pausing to glance around, Tom raced for the tunnel that would take him back through the storage caves and out into daylight.

He ran past the web-shrouded

barrels, hearing the enraged Beast
scuttling along behind, catching up
on him all too quickly on his eight
scissoring legs.

At last Tom saw sunlight, and burst
out into the open. He was relieved to
be out of those stifling dark tunnels,
but lightning was forking across the
empty sky.

Tom saw his Aunt in the distance
on the path to the village, stumbling
along as quickly as she could.
Moments later, he heard a rattling
noise behind him and a harsh hiss
of breath.

He spun around, sword and shield
ready as Kama emerged from the
cave mouth. The Beast's human head
bowed to stoop under the lintel, his
hideous spider body and legs oozing
slowly out through the entrance in a

way that made Tom's stomach turn.

Letting out a high-pitched shriek, Kama scuttled forwards, the whip curling above his head. Even in the fresh air, the Beast reeked, and the running sores and burn-wounds on his body seeped clotted gore.

What did that to the Beast? Tom wondered. *Was it anything to do with my father?*

Then a breath of wind lifted the lank black hair from the Beast's face, and Tom saw a hideous sight.

Except for that one evil black eye, the Beast had no face! The eye-socket was ribbed and ridged with scar tissue, as though something had tried to gouge the eye out. And the other eye was entirely missing, leaving only a cross-shaped scar that was crusted with dry blood. Where the nose

and mouth should have been was a
hideous, gaping anchor-shaped wound
that leaked thick liquid.

Tom stared at the appalling face,
rooted to the spot with horror. Kama
lifted his head and a horrible noise
came from the ragged wound where
his mouth should have been.

He swung his whip, and Tom
flung himself sideways as the Beast's

weapon scored a deep furrow in the ground. Scrambling quickly to his feet, Tom noticed a long diagonal wound that ran down the Beast's human-looking chest.

It looks like an old sword wound that has never healed.

Perhaps that's the Beast's weakness. If I can score a hit there with my sword, I might be able to defeat Kama. He lunged forwards, aiming for the wound with his sword. But Kama was as quick as a striking serpent. He lashed out with one huge arm, lifting Tom off his feet and sending him crashing to the ground.

The Faceless Beast was on him in a moment, forelegs rearing, the scarred mouth spraying pus as he shrieked, the whip whistling through the air.

Tom cried out in pain and arched

his back as the whip spun around his waist. The Beast hoisted him into the air. Tom struggled furiously, but his sword and shield were torn from his grip. Weaponless, he hung in the air above the Beast's head as the loathsome face turned up towards him. The mouth slit widened to reveal broken, snapping fangs.

I have to get free…

Tom writhed in mid-air, twisting to uncoil the whip. It worked! The snaking web came loose. Using skills honed in dozens of deadly battles, Tom spun himself around as he fell – and landed upright on the spider's back, his legs straddling the huge body.

He lunged forwards, wrapping his arms around Kama's thick throat and his legs around its torso. He clung on grimly, crossing his ankles, tightening

his hold as the Beast lurched from side
to side to try and throw him off.

Fighting to keep on the Beast's back,
he caught a glimpse of Silver and
Storm racing towards them.

They've come back to help, but what can they do against such a terrible Beast?

Kama heaved and jerked, fighting to shake Tom off as the two animals hurried forwards. The Beast's arms strained back as Tom swung his body to and fro, ducking his head to avoid being caught by Kama's raking fingers.

Storm came to a clattering halt as he caught sight of the terrible Beast, and even Silver, the bravest of wolves, dropped to his stomach, snarling but not daring to move any closer.

But where's Elenna?

No sooner had the thought passed through Tom's mind than his friend came racing out of the cave mouth, carrying a length of rope she must have found inside.

While Tom struggled to stay on Kama's heaving back, Elenna ran to Storm and tied one end of the rope to his saddle. Then she sprinted over to Silver and placed the other end of the rope between the wolf's jaws.

Tom felt he had an inkling of what she was planning. But with every moment, his grip on Kama's back was loosening. The Beast's neck was arching, the muscles standing up like ropes as he twisted his head, his hideous mouth gaping to reveal the deadly fangs.

"Quickly, Elenna!" Tom shouted. "I can't hold on much longer!"

CHAPTER SIX

AN EMPTY VICTORY

The Beast wrenched his head from side to side as he battled to fling Tom off. But Tom refused to give in, even though his muscles ached for release and the stench of burnt flesh filled his head and made him dizzy.

He saw Elenna leap into Storm's saddle and urge him towards Tom and the Beast. Silver loped along at their side, then, at a cry from Elenna, the wolf angled away and the rope was drawn taut between them.

It's now or never!

Tom released his legs from around Kama's chest and planted his feet firmly on the back of the spider body. The Beast shook himself, his eight crooked legs stabbing the ground, and his arms reaching back to try and drag Tom off.

But Tom still had a tight chokehold around the Beast's neck, and although the lank, stinking hair was in his face, he could still see the two animals approaching with the rope stretched between them.

Calling on the strength gifted to him by the breastplate of the Golden Armour, Tom dug his feet into the Beast's back and wrenched Kama's neck around, forcing him to scuttle to the side, like a wild horse that needed taming.

Silver and Storm ran either side of the Beast.

The rope caught against Kama's forelegs with a loud twanging sound. Tom felt the jolt as the Beast's legs were yanked from underneath him.

Storm was brought up sharp by the impact and Elenna only just managed to stay in the saddle. Silver's head was dragged to the side and he almost flipped over as the Beast's legs became tangled up.

Kama stumbled and fell, crashing to the ground as Tom leaped clear.

Tom landed neatly on his feet. Kama lay on his back shrieking, his jointed legs thrashing in the air and his fists thumping the ground.

Tom smiled grimly as he realised that Elenna's plan had succeeded even better than he had hoped. Kama writhed and squirmed, clawing up clods of earth with his hands as he fought desperately to get onto his legs again. But like any spider turned on its back, the gruesome Beast was helpless.

"Tom! Take your sword!" called Elenna, leaping down from Storm's back and throwing his sword towards him. He snatched it out of the air and stood over the Beast.

As he lifted his sword he paused, seeing that the long diagonal wound on Kama's chest was now seeping a putrid green vapour. It smelled so unbearably foul that Tom was forced to take a step backwards.

Keeping his sword ready, Tom reached into his tunic and took out the ruby of Torgor. Gripping it in his fist he stared into the Beast's ghastly single eye, wanting to make himself understood.

"Kama, hear me," he said. "Why must the son of Taladon die?"

Kama's horrible mouth opened in a grimace that revealed his broken teeth. But he made no sound.

"Kama! Speak to me!" Tom
shouted.

He was forced further back as
the green vapour began to surge
out of the wound in thick clouds.

The vapour shrouded the Beast, enveloping it so that Tom could no longer see it.

Then, slowly, the smoke vanished.

The Beast was gone.

Tom dropped to his knees, exhaustion overwhelming him as his sword slipped from his fingers.

The Beast disappeared without telling me the truth about my father.

Elenna ran up to him. "Are you hurt?" she asked.

He looked up at her. "No," he said softly. "But this isn't the end of the Quest. We still need to find Kensa and Sanpao."

"Tom!" It was Uncle Henry's voice, calling to him. Tom struggled to his feet. His uncle and aunt were hurrying along the path from the village. Henry was holding a hammer.

"I thought your uncle might be able to help you," said Aunt Maria as they came up to him.

"There is something you can do," Tom said wearily. "I need to know why these Lightning Beasts are so determined to kill the son of Taladon."

His uncle and aunt shared an uneasy look, refusing to look him in the eye.

"If you know the truth, you must tell me," Tom insisted.

"I hoped you might never need to be told," said Uncle Henry. "But we can't hide it from you. The reason is..."

Even as his uncle began to explain, Tom felt an invisible force wrench at his body. He was lifted up off the ground and held suspended high above the rooftops of Errinel. He gasped, seeing Elenna hanging helplessly at his side.

"What's happening?" she panted.

"Magic!" said Tom, and a moment later they were engulfed by a whirling cloud of dust.

Tom felt firm ground under his feet as the dust-cloud evaporated.

He looked around, recognising the courtroom of the Circle of Wizards. This was the place where their friend Aduro had been put on trial and condemned.

Tom spun round at the echoing crash of a gavel. He stared up in shock and alarm. Aduro was hovering above the centre of the circular chamber, his arms and legs stretched out, his wrists and ankles shackled with green glowing bonds.

The Judge sat in his chair, his face grim and merciless.

"Your time is up," he boomed, glaring at Tom and Elenna. "You were sent to capture the sorceress Kensa and Sanpao the Pirate King." His voice roared in Tom's ears. "You have failed! Do you have anything to say for yourselves before I pass Aduro's final sentence?"

CHAPTER SEVEN

THE ULTIMATE SACRIFICE

Tom lifted his chin and looked straight into the Judge's cold, hard eyes.

"I do have something to tell you," he said loudly, his voice echoing around the ancient Court of Wizards. The Judge glared at him, his face unyielding.

You don't scare me! I've defeated worse

creatures than you, Tom thought.

"I was the one who travelled the Lightning Path," Tom said firmly. "So it is my fault that the Lightning Beasts were set loose to ravage the three kingdoms."

The Judge banged his fist on the

table before him. "Of what interest is that to this Court?" he demanded.

"It was my duty to find the Beasts and to defeat them," continued Tom, undaunted. "It's true I turned from the hunt for Kensa and Sanpao, but only because of the harm the Beasts could have done if they were not stopped." He gave the Judge a fierce look. "Could anyone else have conquered the Beasts? Could you?"

"Another remark like that and you will regret it!" shouted the Judge.

"I apologise," said Tom. "But it was the code of honour given to me by Aduro that guided my actions." He looked up at his friend, hanging helplessly below the domed ceiling. His eyes met Aduro's and he saw gratitude in them. Aduro knew he had done the right thing. "I put the safety of the three kingdoms and of their people above everything else," Tom said. "And I would do it again in a heartbeat."

He held his breath as he awaited the Judge's response. He heard muttering from the other wizards. There were scornful shouts but also a few mumbled words of agreement. From the corner of his eye, Tom could see Elenna, standing stiffly at his side, her face drawn and anxious.

"I'm proud of you," Elenna whispered. "That was exactly the right thing to say."

"I just hope I haven't made things worse," Tom murmured back.

The Judge leaned forwards over his high bench and the courtroom became silent. His brows lowered and his eyes became slits. "You have proved yourself a worthy champion, it cannot be denied," he said. "But the fact remains that you were charged by this Court with a task that you have failed to complete."

Tom braced himself, wondering what was coming.

"Because of this, the sorceress Kensa and Sanpao the Pirate King are still at large," continued the Judge. "And information has just reached us that they are in Avantia itself." He pointed up towards the suspended wizard. "All of this has happened because Aduro broke the ancient law forbidding the use of the Lightning Paths."

"But he only did it to save the people of Henkrall!" cried Tom.

"Silence!" thundered the Judge. "It is clear to us that the shamed wizard mentored you well. Without you and your companions, the three kingdoms may well have faced utter ruin." He looked up at Aduro. "We have taken this into account when coming to our verdict," he said. "The prisoner may go free..."

Delight burst in Tom's heart.

"On one condition," continued the Judge. "He must consent to surrender all of his magical powers to the Circle of Wizards."

Tom's spirits crashed at these terrible words.

"Aduro will be a wizard no more. That is our verdict!" the Judge struck the gavel a final time.

"Aduro has always protected this kingdom," cried Elenna. "How can you do this to him?"

Tom took half a step forwards, his

hand moving instinctively to his
sword hilt.

I can't let this happen.

"Peace, my friends," came Aduro's
frail, weary voice from above them.
"Tom, do nothing rash. The law is the
law and I will abide by its rulings."
He looked down at the Judge, a
regretful smile flickering on his lips. "I
have been Avantia's Chief Wizard for
many years now, perhaps this is the
perfect time for me to relinquish my
powers." He bowed his head. "Carry
out your sentence, My Lord."

"No!" shouted Tom, stunned by
Aduro's decision. "You mustn't!"

But even as he spoke, the Judge
rose from his seat and extended his
hand. A streak of purple smoke jetted
out from his palm, striking Aduro in
the chest.

Aduro let out a weak cry, his body
straining in the magical bonds. Tom
watched in shock and disbelief as
a bright blue light seeped from his
friend's body. It was the essence of

the Good Wizard's magic, being taken by the Judge.

In helping Tom, Aduro had paid the ultimate price.

CHAPTER EIGHT

AN OLD ENEMY RETURNS

Tom watched in dismay as the blue light left Aduro's body. It swirled into the purple smoke coming from the Judge's hand and was swallowed up.

The magical shackles holding Aduro spread-eagled in the air dissolved. The wizard floated to the ground and fell onto his knees with a gasp.

Tom and Elenna rushed to his side

and helped him up.

"I'm so sorry," Tom said, looking into Aduro's pale, lined face. For the first time, he looked to Tom like a tired old man. "This is all my fault. I let you down."

"Nonsense, my boy," croaked Aduro. "You did no such thing." He looked keenly into Tom's face. "You have never let me down, and you never could."

Tom felt a lump growing in his throat at his old friend's bravery. But he was used to Aduro being full of magic – with that gone, things could never be the same again.

"One last thing," said the Judge.

Tom turned furiously on him. "Haven't you done enough harm already?" he snapped.

The Judge's face was expressionless as clapped his hands together. "Now that sentence has been passed, certain things can be returned to you," he said.

Tom felt his shield quiver on his back. He pulled it off and saw that the six tokens from his very first Quest had been restored to the face of the shield.

"Tom, your belt!" cried Elenna.

Sure enough, the belt with the six jewels in it had appeared around his waist, with Torgor's ruby set in its usual place among the others.

The Judge had given back the powers that had been taken from him. Tom ran his fingers over the familiar tokens. He had missed their powers in his Quest and he had longed for their return. But now he had them once more, there was no sense of triumph. Aduro's huge sacrifice made this small victory seem empty and hollow.

"Go now!" demanded the Judge. "This court dismisses you."

With a wave of his hand, the courtroom vanished.

Tom and Elenna were in the King's throne room, sitting slumped by the throne while Aduro and his young apprentice Daltec stood facing the King.

"You must now take on the role of Chief Wizard of Avantia, Daltec," said King Hugo.

Daltec looked nervously at him. "But I am young and my powers are not yet fully tested, Sire," he mumbled.

Aduro patted him on the back. "Do not fear," he said. "You will become a fine and learned sorcerer." He gestured towards Tom and Elenna. "And you will help these brave young people as well as I ever could."

Tom wasn't so sure, but he said

nothing – Daltec looked unhappy enough as it was.

"But am I not King in Avantia?" growled King Hugo. "How can it be that a mere Judge can overrule my wishes and remove my Chief Wizard without my permission?"

"Peace, Sire," Aduro said gently. "Even a King must abide by the ancient and sacred laws of magic."

"But those laws can corrupt," said a high-pitched voice that sounded strangely

familiar to Tom's ears. He jumped up, sword in hand as a round, pale face appeared at the throne room doors.

"Petra!" he shouted, immediately recognising the young witch who had once been the Evil Wizard Malvel's eager assistant. She had changed since he had seen her last, her lank brown hair was now streaked with grey and her face showed none of the cruelty and cunning that he remembered.

"Yes, it is I," she said, coming into the room. "But you won't need your sword." She flung out her arm and twirled her fingers in the air. Instantly, Tom felt his sword arm grow numb and stiff.

She's more powerful and dangerous than before, he thought as the coldness seeped up to his shoulder.

Elenna reached for her bow, but Petra's hand moved again and Elenna was frozen instantly where she sat.

"What is the meaning of this?" demanded King Hugo, standing up.

"I have not come here to do harm," Petra said. "I want to help you." She made another gesture with her hand and both Tom and Elenna were able to move again. "There," Petra said. "If you don't trust me, do as you will."

Tom sheathed his sword. "Just tell us why you're here," he said.

Petra walked towards the throne. "You have been deceived," she said. "The truth has been staring you in the face, and none of you saw it." She turned towards one of the large wall tapestries, lifting her hands and muttering under her breath.

As Tom watched, the design on the tapestry began to warp and change into a strange, vivid picture.

They saw Kensa and Sanpao on board the flying pirate ship. It was night and the uneasy allies were arguing angrily. But as Tom and the others watched, they became silent. A tall, hooded figure had appeared on the deck.

"How did you allow the boy to defeat all six of the Lightning Beasts?" growled the figure in a deep, scratchy voice.

"Forgive me, lord," cried Kensa, falling to her knees.

Tom's eyes widened in amazement as the proud and fierce Pirate King also dropped to one knee in front of the hooded figure.

"Who is that man?" asked Elenna.

"Hush and all will be revealed," snapped Petra.

"I am your humble servant," said Sanpao. "What would you have us do?"

The figure turned and a shaft of

moonlight fell on the hooded face.

Cold eyes glinted under a heavy brow and the wrinkles around the sour mouth deepened as the thin lips twisted into a smile.

Tom let out a startled gasp. There could be no possible mistake.

The hooded man was the Judge.

CHAPTER NINE

DECEPTION AND DISHONOUR

Tom stumbled towards the tapestry in a daze, pushing past Petra and standing so close to the magical vision that he felt he could reach out and close his fingers around the Judge's throat.

"It was you!" he cried, his heart hammering, his hands balled into fists. "You've been controlling Kensa and

Sanpao from the very start! Everything that has happened is your fault."

He drew his sword in rage, the blade ringing as it left the sheath.

"You cannot fight them," said Petra. "This is just an image I have conjured."

"Where are they?" demanded Tom. "Take me to them."

Petra shook her head. "Listen to what they are saying," she said. "It may help you to understand."

"Do as she says," added Aduro, his face grim as he came up to Tom's side.

Tom focused on the conversation taking place on the pirate ship.

"The boy is a formidable fighter," Sanpao was saying, on his feet again and running a thumb along the blade of his drawn scimitar. "Much as I have sought to open his veins, he's thwarted me at every turn. And for all her magic, Kensa did nothing to help."

"If I was not cursed with such a blundering dolt as a partner, I'd have defeated the boy long ago," snarled Kensa, turning on the Pirate King. "Don't try to blame me for your incompetence."

"Ha!" scoffed Sanpao. "Your magic failed at every turn. Without you getting in my way, I'd have sliced the boy's head clean off at the very start."

"Sliced your own ear off, more like!" spat Kensa. "You are no more than a brutal buffoon!"

"And your magic couldn't turn a tadpole into a toad!" roared Sanpao.

The Judge's voice was a low, menacing growl. "Silence, fools! You bicker and quarrel like whining children!" His eyes glittered fiercely in the moonlight. "Do not seek to lay the blame on each other! I took away all the boy's advantages, and still you could not defeat him."

"His companions help him at every turn," said Kensa. "The girl is a fine warrior, and those two animals – the horse and the wolf – they also play their part in his victories."

"But the boy is the heart of it," said Sanpao. "Destroy him and nothing would stand between us and complete dominion over the three kingdoms!"

"Yes!" cried the Judge. "And at the heart of the boy is his faith and resolve! His faith in his father and his resolve to tread in Taladon's footsteps." A cruel smile split the Judge's face. "That faith and that resolve had to be broken if we were to weaken the boy. That is why I allowed him to keep the ruby of Torgor."

"Of course," said Kensa, her green eyes glowing. "You made sure he could communicate with the Beasts."

"I do not understand," said Sanpao. "What of it?"

"Witless brute!" snapped Kensa. "Do you not see? The boy had to learn that his father defeated the Lightning Beasts using dishonourable methods

and low deception."

Understanding appeared on Sanpao's tattooed face. "The boy thinks he has been walking in a hero's tracks," he said. "But his feet will falter now that he has learned that his father was less of a hero than he believed." A roar of vicious laughter erupted from his mouth. "I like it!"

Tom trembled with shame and anger as he listened to Sanpao's mocking laughter. To think that his father had acted badly hurt more than the deepest battle wound.

A gentle hand rested on his shoulder. He turned and found himself gazing into Aduro's wise eyes.

"Is it true?" Tom asked, his voice trembling. "My uncle was about to tell me something when we were brought to the Wizard's courtroom. I remember

the look in his eyes. It was the look
of someone with a terrible secret."

"Not even the greatest hero can
avoid making mistakes sometimes,"
Aduro told him. "The true measure
of a hero is that he learns from those
mistakes and atones for them. Your
father was very young when he
had to face the six Beasts you have

just vanquished. It was the most dangerous time of his life – the hardest Beast Quest he ever undertook." The old man's face was full of kindness. "Taladon chose to imprison the Beasts in the Lightning because he believed it was the only way to keep the kingdom safe," Aduro continued. "But not a day passed when he did not question his actions and regret what he had done."

Tom bowed his head. "I see," he said quietly. He had always looked up to his father – it was hard and confusing to learn that the Master of Beasts was flawed.

The Judge's voice pulled him out of his dark thoughts and he turned again to look at the vision that Petra had conjured.

"I come to you straight from the Court of the Circle of Wizards," the

Judge said gloatingly to Kensa and Sanpao. "Aduro is a wizard no more! His powers have been drained from him."

"Excellent," hissed Kensa. "And with him out of the way, we have made a great stride closer to unseating the King and taking over his realm."

Sanpao's raucous laughter echoed again. "And then we will raise an Avantian army and lead it to the conquest of Gwildor!"

"And after Gwildor, Kayonia!" cried Kensa.

The Judge spread his arms so that his cloak opened out like black wings. "And there will be no one with the power to stop us!" he snarled. "All the kingdoms shall be ours!"

And then, as Tom watched in horror, the Judge drew a long gleaming sword from beneath his cloak. His eyes turned towards Tom and he reached out with the sharp blade.

"Ahh!" Tom let out a cry of shock and pain as the tip of the sword came through the tapestry and cut a thin line across his cheek.

"Let the great conquest of the realms begin now!" the Judge roared as Tom felt the blood trickling down his face.

And at that moment, Tom realised that he was no longer standing in King Hugo's throne room. He and the others had been magically transported aboard Sanpao's ship.

"Kill them!" bellowed the Judge. "Kill them all!"

CHAPTER TEN

THE DEADLIEST FOE

Tom stared around himself in a daze as he felt the pirate ship's deck under his feet and saw the moonlit faces of his enemies turn towards him in triumph. The Judge's powers were truly terrible.

And he saw that the Judge's sorcery had brought Elenna and the others on board as well.

The laughing Pirate King bore down on Tom with his scimitar raised above his head. Sparks crackled from Kensa's fingers and the Judge's huge sword whistled through the air.

Behind them, Sanpao's pirate crew was pouring from the ship's hatches, armed and howling for blood.

"Petra, Daltec!" Tom shouted, taking control in an instant. "Fight the Judge!" He spun around to where King Hugo and Elenna stood looking stunned. "Sire, you and Elenna must try to hold Kensa off – I'm going to stop Sanpao!"

He saw Aduro standing among them, his hands raised for conjuring as though he had forgotten for a moment that he no longer had any powers. "And protect Aduro!"

Tom ducked as Sanpao's scimitar scythed the air above his head. He hurled himself forwards to trip the

pirate. But Sanpao was a canny
fighter – he leaped over Tom, slashing
downwards as he went. Tom's shield
warded off the blow and he was on
his feet in a moment.

They faced one another, circling
slowly, searching for weaknesses.

"I'm going to slice you open, boy,"
mocked Sanpao. "I'll turn you inside
out and wear your guts as a belt!"

Sanpao lunged, but Tom deflected

the curved blade with a sideways thrust of his shield.

"I don't think my guts would fit around that big belly of yours!" Tom retorted, jabbing with his sword. As Sanpao's scimitar whipped around to parry, Tom spun and launched a fierce kick to the pirate's midriff.

Grunting with pain, Sanpao staggered backwards, colliding with Kensa just as she unleashed a powerful spell at King Hugo and Elenna. The spell went wild, striking half a dozen pirates and knocking them off their feet.

"You clumsy oaf!" shrieked Kensa, hurling a dazzling spell at Sanpao. Blinded for the moment, the Pirate King staggered across the deck, swinging wildly with his scimitar.

An arrow sped from Elenna's bow,

as King Hugo aimed a blow at Kensa's legs. The sorceress jumped back with an angry shriek, only just avoiding the sweeping blade as the arrow grazed past her shoulder.

Close by, Daltec and Petra were dancing around the tall, dreadful figure of the Judge, casting spells that came at him from all directions, cracking and exploding in a dazzle of bright lights. But none of the spells seemed to reach the Judge, and he flung bolts of purple lightning from his palms that burst like thunder all over the ship.

Tom saw Daltec knocked off his feet by one of the Judge's spells and was sent spinning across the deck, knocking pirates over like skittles as he went. Petra let out a yell as coils of purple smoke wound around her, pinning her arms to her sides and lifting her into the air. The Judge was proving far too powerful for them in a battle of sorceries. But for the moment he had his back turned to Tom.

"For Aduro!" Tom snarled. He dodged past the blundering Pirate King, still hacking blindly around himself with his scimitar, and flung himself at the Judge, his sword aimed at the treacherous man's heart.

But the Judge proved to be as quick as the lightning bolts that shot from his fingers. He whirled to face Tom, his sword chiming as it warded off the blow.

"Enough of this!" roared the Judge, his eyes blazing as he raised his arms high above his head. "Let the Fangs of the Wild Wind be Unleashed!"

The very air around the Judge seemed to ripple as he spoke the incantation. Tom felt a wave of invisible force strike him, sweeping him off his feet and hurling him head over heels across the ship.

As he spun helplessly in the force of the spell, Tom saw that it had also struck Elenna and Petra and the others, lifting them into the night sky like storm-blown feathers. Moments later, Tom and his companions were sent tumbling over the side of the ship.

Far below, Tom saw King Hugo's castle, shrouded in the shadows of night. The flying pirate ship was hovering over Avantia's capital city.

They hung there for the space of three or four heartbeats, then the spell released them and they plummeted towards the ground.

But Tom kept calm. He had Arcta's feather on his shield again – a magical token that had saved him from deadly

falls in the past. Twisting himself
nimbly as he plunged earthwards, he
caught hold of Elenna's sleeve, calling
on the power of the feather to slow
their descent.

He could see that Petra and Daltec had
managed to conjure a shimmering cloud-
cushion, and that Aduro and the King
were being supported on it with them

as it floated downwards in wide circles.

The six of them landed safely in the castle courtyard.

"Is everyone all right?" Tom asked.

"Yes," panted Daltec, helping Aduro to his feet. "All are safe!"

Tom stared up into the sky. Sanpao's great galleon was silhouetted against the full moon. Even as he watched, the blood-red sails billowed and the ship sped off across the sky, vanishing as swiftly as a shooting star.

Tom raised his fist angrily. "Run while you can!" he shouted. "But know this – while there is blood in my veins I will follow you, even if it takes me to the very ends of the world and beyond! In the name of my father, Taladon the Swift, Master of Beasts – I will track you down and defeat you!"

Join Tom on the next stage
of the Beast Quest!

Win an exclusive
Beast Quest T-shirt and goody bag!

In every Beast Quest book the Beast Quest logo is
hidden in one of the pictures. Find the logos in books
67 to 72 and make a note of which pages they appear
on. Write the six page numbers on a postcard and
send it in to us.
Each month we will draw one winner to receive
a Beast Quest T-shirt and goody bag.

THE BEAST QUEST COMPETITION:
The Darkest Hour
Orchard Books
338 Euston Road, London NW1 3BH
Australian readers should email:
childrens.books@hachette.com.au

New Zealand readers should write to:
Beast Quest Competition
4 Whetu Place, Mairangi Bay, Auckland, NZ
or email: childrensbooks@hachette.co.nz

Only one entry per child.
Final draw: January 2014

You can also enter this competition
via the Beast Quest website: www.beastquest.co.uk

Join the Quest,
Join the Tribe

www.beastquest.co.uk

Have you checked out the Beast Quest website?
It's the place to go for games, downloads, activities,
sneak previews and lots of fun!

You can read all about your favourite Beasts,
download free screensavers and desktop wallpapers
for your computer, and even challenge your friends
to a Beast Tournament.

Sign up to the newsletter at www.beastquest.co.uk
to receive exclusive extra content and the
opportunity to enter special members-only
competitions. We'll send you up-to-date info on all
the Beast Quest books, including the next exciting
series which features six brand-new Beasts!

Get 30% off all Beast Quest Books at www.beastquest.co.uk
Enter the code BEAST at the checkout.

All books priced at £4.99.
Special bumper editions priced at £5.99.

Orchard Books are available from all good bookshops, or can
be ordered from our website: www.orchardbooks.co.uk,
or telephone 01235 827702, or fax 01235 8227703.

Series 12: THE DARKEST HOUR
COLLECT THEM ALL!

Three lands are in terrible danger from six new
Beasts. Tom must ride to the rescue!

978 1 40832 396 0

978 1 40832 397 7

978 1 40832 398 4

978 1 40832 399 1

978 1 40832 400 4

978 1 40832 401 1

NEW ADAM BLADE SERIES

Read on for an exclusive extract of
CEPHALOX THE CYBERSQUID!

THE MERRYN TOUCH

The water was up to Max's knees and still rising. Soon it would reach his waist. Then his chest. Then his face.

I'm going to die down here, he thought.

He hammered on the dome with all his strength, but the plexiglass held firm.

Then he saw something pale looming through the dark water outside the submersible. A long, silvery spike. It must be the squid-creature, with one of its weird robotic attachments. Any second now it would smash the glass and finish him off...

There was a crash. The sub rocked. The silver spike thrust through the broken plexiglass. More water surged in. Then the spike withdrew and the water poured in faster. Max forced his way against the torrent to the opening. If he could just squeeze through the gap...

The jet of water pushed him back. He took one last deep breath, and then the water was over his head.

He clamped his mouth shut, struggling forwards, feeling the pressure on his lungs build.

Something gripped his arms, but it wasn't the squid's tentacle – it was a pair of hands, pulling him through the hole. The broken plexiglass scraped his sides and then he was through.

The monster was nowhere to be seen. In the dim underwater light, he made out the face of his rescuer. It was the Merryn girl, and next to her was a large silver swordfish.

She smiled at him.

Max couldn't smile back. He'd been saved from a metal coffin, only to swap it for a watery one. The pressure of the ocean squeezed him on every side. His lungs felt as though they were bursting.

He thrashed his limbs, rising upwards. He looked to where he thought the surface was, but saw nothing, only endless water. His cheeks puffed with the effort to hold in air. He let some of it out slowly, but it only made him want to breathe in more.

He knew he had no chance. He was too deep, he'd never make it to the surface in time. Soon he'd no longer be able to hold his breath. The water would swirl into his lungs and he'd die here, at the bottom of the sea. *Just like my mother*, he thought.

The Merryn girl rose up beside him, reached out and put her hands on his neck. Warmth seemed to flow from her fingers. Then the warmth turned to pain. What was happening? It got worse and worse, until Max felt as if his throat was being ripped open. Was she trying to kill him?

———

He struggled in panic, trying to push her off. His mouth opened and water rushed in.

That was it. He was going to die.

Then he realised something – the water was cool and sweet. He sucked it down into his lungs. Nothing had ever tasted so good.

He was breathing underwater!

He put his hands to his neck and found two soft, gill-like openings where the Merryn girl had touched him. His eyes widened in astonishment.

The girl smiled.

Other strange things were happening. Max found he could see more clearly. The water seemed lighter and thinner. He made out the shapes of underwater plants, rock formations and shoals of fish in the distance, which had been invisible before. And he didn't feel as if the ocean was crushing him any more.

Is this what it's like to be a Merryn? he wondered.

"I'm Lia," said the girl. "And this is Spike." She patted the swordfish on the back and it nuzzled against her.

"Hi, I'm Max." He clapped his hand to his mouth in shock. He was speaking the same strange language of sighs and whistles he'd heard the girl use when he first met her – but now it made sense, as if he was born to speak it.

"What have you done to me?" he said.

"Saved your life," said Lia. "You're welcome, by the way."

"Oh – don't think I'm not grateful – I am. But – you've turned me into a Merryn?"

The girl laughed. "Not exactly, but I've given you some Merryn powers. You can breathe underwater, speak our language, and your senses are much stronger. Come on – we need to get away from here. The Cyber Squid may come back."

In one graceful movement she slipped onto Spike's back. Max clambered on behind her.

"Hold tight," Lia said. "Spike – let's go!"

Max put his arms around the Merryn's waist. He was jerked backwards as the swordfish shot off through the water, but he managed to hold on.

They raced above underwater forests of gently waving fronds, and hills and valleys of rock. Max saw giant crabs scuttling over the seabed. Undersea creatures loomed up – jellyfish, an octopus, a school of dolphins – but Spike nimbly swerved round them.

"Where are we going?" Max asked.

"You'll see," Lia said over her shoulder.

"I need to find my dad," Max said. The crazy things that had happened in the last few moments had driven his father from his mind. Now it all came flooding back. Was his dad gone for good? "We have to do something! That monster's got my dad – and my dogbot too!"

"It's not the Cyber Squid who wants your father. It's the Professor who's *controlling* the Cyber Squid. I tried to warn you back at the city – but you wouldn't listen."

"I didn't understand you then!"

"You Breathers don't try to understand – that's your whole problem!"

"I'm trying now. What is that monster? And who is the Professor?"

"I'll explain everything when we arrive."

"Arrive where?"

The seabed suddenly fell away. A steep valley sloped down, leading way, way deeper than the ocean ridge Aquora was built on. The swordfish dived. The water grew darker.

Far below, Max saw a faint yellow glimmer. As he watched it grew bigger and brighter, until it became a vast undersea city of golden-glinting rock rushing up towards them. There were towers, spires, domes, bridges, courtyards, squares, gardens. A city as big as Aquora, and far more beautiful, at the bottom of the sea.

———

Max gasped in amazement. The water was
dark, but the city emitted a glow of its own
– a warm phosphorescent light that spilled
from the many windows. The rock sparkled.

Orange, pink and scarlet corals and seashells decorated the walls in intricate patterns.

"This is – amazing!" he said.

Lia turned round and smiled at him. "It's my home," she said. "Sumara!"

Calling all Adam Blade Fans!
We need YOU!

Are you a huge fan of Beast Quest? Is Adam Blade your favourite author? Do you want to know more about his new series, Sea Quest, before anybody else IN THE WORLD?

We're looking for 100 of the most loyal Adam Blade fans to become Sea Quest Cadets.

So how do I become a Sea Quest Cadet?

Simply go to **www.seaquestbooks.co.uk** and fill in the form.

What do I get if I become a Sea Quest Cadet?

You will be one of a limited number of people to receive exclusive Sea Quest merchandise.

What do I have to do as a Sea Quest Cadet?

Take part in Sea Quest activities with your friends!

ENROL TODAY!
SEA QUEST NEEDS YOU!

Open to UK and Republic of Ireland residents only.